Champion's New Shoes

Look for all
the books in the

PET RESCUE CLUB
series

ASPCA kids

PET RESCUE CLUB

Champion's New Shoes

By Brenda Scott Royce

Cover Illustration by Steve James

Studio Fun International
An imprint of Printers Row Publishing Group
A division of Readerlink Distribution Services, LLC
10350 Barnes Canyon Road, Suite 100, San Diego, CA 92121
www.studiofun.com

All notations of errors or omissions should be addressed to
Studio Fun International, Editorial Department, at the above address.

ISBN 978-0-7944-3998-9

Manufactured, printed, and assembled in the United States of America.
21 20 19 18 17 1 2 3 4 5

Library of Congress Cataloging-in-Publication Data is available on request.

***The American Society for the Prevention of Cruelty to Animals® (ASPCA®) will
receive 5% - 7% from the sale of ASPCA products, with a minimum guarantee of
$25,000, through December 2017.**

Comments? Questions? Call us at: 1-888-217-3346

To Nic

—*B. S. R*

1

Zach the Mind Reader

"Earth to Adam." Janey Whitfield looked up from her tablet computer at her friend Adam Santos. "Are you even listening?"

Janey and Adam and their friends Lolli Simpson and Zach Goldman were having a meeting of the Pet Rescue Club at Adam's house. Janey was reading them an e-mail she received from a girl at their school. Lolli and Zach were all ears, but Adam's mind seemed to be somewhere else.

Adam was staring out his bedroom window at the house next door. A large moving van was parked in the driveway. "Sorry I got distracted," he told his friends when he caught them staring at him. "I'm just super curious about my new neighbors." Adam was normally very responsible. Even though he was only nine years old, he had his own successful dog walking business in town. "Read it again, Janey. I promise to pay attention this time."

Janey was sitting at Adam's desk with her tablet propped in front of her. "It's from Stacey Fletcher, a fifth grader," she said, before reading the e-mail aloud.

I got a hamster for my birthday and named him Hammie. Hammie was great but I was worried he'd get lonely when I was at school and soccer practice. So I got him a friend, Herman. Things were fine until Herman had babies—six of them! My hamster habitat isn't big enough for eight hamsters, and my parents say I can only keep one. Can you help me find homes for the rest?

Janey looked up from her tablet. "What do you think?"

Zach was stretched out on Adam's bed, while Lolli sat cross-legged on the floor. "I think Herman is a weird name for a girl hamster," Zach said, laughing.

Janey shrugged. "I guess Stacey thought it was a boy."

Lolli nodded. "Sounds like a great case for the Pet Rescue Club!"

The four friends had started the club after finding a neglected dog named Truman a new home. Since then, they'd helped lots of other animals, including a cat, a pony, and even a dog who needed an operation. They also reunited several missing pets with their worried owners after a big storm hit.

"I concur!" Janey said. She loved finding interesting words and using them whenever she could. "Concur" was her new favorite way of saying she agreed. "What do you think, Adam?"

"I think . . . " Adam's gaze had drifted out the window again. He watched an older woman carry a large potted plant toward the empty house. "It would be so awesome if they have kids my age."

"The hamsters?" Lolli asked.

"What? No, my new neighbors." Adam turned back to his friends. "I wonder if they have any pets."

"I know how to read minds, you know." Zach removed a small blanket from the foot of Adam's bed and wrapped it around his shoulders like a cape. He looked like a magician in a bad movie. "So I can tell you all about your new neighbors."

Lolli and Janey exchanged disbelieving looks.

"Really?" Adam didn't try to hide the doubt in his voice. Zach liked to tease and joke around. This was probably just another one of his gags.

"Watch this." Zach stood facing the

window. He put his hands to his temples and fluttered his eyelids. He spoke as though he was in a trance. "Their name is . . . Butterfield. They have a son who is away at college. And a cat—no, a dog. A dog named Digger! And they're tired."

Lolli, Adam, and Janey peered out the window. The moving van was pulling away. The older woman Adam saw earlier was standing on the sidewalk, waving good-bye to the driver. A man with silver hair and a trim beard was carrying a large box into the house. Dozens more boxes were stacked by the front door.

"Of course they're tired," Janey said. "Look at all those boxes!"

Adam adjusted his glasses. "I don't see a dog."

"Zach's just goofing," said Lolli. "He can't possibly know all that stuff about them."

Janey returned to the desk and picked up her tablet. "I'll send an e-mail to Stacey, saying that we will help solve her hamster problem. Do we all concur?"

Zach made a face. "Can't you just say 'agree' like a normal person?"

Adam plopped into a beanbag chair. "Janey is normal," he told Zach. "You're the one wearing a blanket cape and pretending to read minds."

Janey drafted the e-mail and clicked SEND just as the doorbell rang.

Adam scrambled to his feet. He loved when people came to his house. "I wonder who that is." He reached the living room as his mother was opening the front door. Standing on the stoop were his new neighbors.

"Hello," the man said. "I'm Bernie Butterfield. My wife Betty and I just moved in next door, and we wanted to introduce ourselves."

Adam's mouth fell open upon hearing the name Butterfield. Could it be true? Did Zach really read their minds?

Janey and Lolli had followed Adam to the front door, but Zach was too busy doubled over with laughter to join them.

Adam's mother spoke first. "I'm Lenore Santos, and this is my son Adam. Welcome to the neighborhood! Please, come inside."

"Just for a moment," Mrs. Butterfield said. "We have a lot of unpacking to do!"

"We saw you moving in," Adam said, shaking hands with the Butterfields. "I was wondering . . . do you have kids? Or pets?"

Mrs. Butterfield smiled and nodded. "Our son, Neil, is away at college, and we have one dog. We put him in the backyard so he wouldn't bother the movers."

Adam, Janey, and Lolli were wide-eyed with wonder. Zach was right about everything!

"Adam is great with dogs," Mrs. Santos said. "He has his own dog-walking business. And he started a Pet Rescue Club with his friends. They were just having a meeting." She introduced the Butterfields to Janey and Lolli, but Zach was nowhere to be seen.

As she shook hands with the Butterfields, Janey asked, "What's your dog's name?" She let out a gasp when Mr. Butterfield responded, "Digger."

2

New Neighbors

Zach staggered into the living room, laughing uncontrollably. "What a great prank!" He pointed at his three friends. "You should see your faces!"

Mrs. Butterfield smiled in recognition. "Hello, Zach."

"You know him?" Adam asked his new neighbor.

"I knew it!" Janey glared at Zach. "You tricked us."

When he finally stopped giggling, Zach

explained that he'd been on his way to Adam's house when he saw the Butterfields moving in next door. He introduced himself and asked them for an empty box for his cat. "Mulberry loves to play in boxes," he told the group. He pointed to the spot where he'd left the box—along with his backpack and skateboard—upon entering Adam's house. He finished his story, "Then they told me about their son and their dog."

Janey told the Butterfields, "He pretended he'd read your minds!" She rolled her eyes, thinking how close she'd come to believing in Zach's psychic abilities.

"He also said you were tired," Lolli added, concern in her voice.

Mrs. Santos stepped forward. "You poor dears. Please, come sit down. Can I offer you some water? Or lemonade?"

"Oh no, thank you, we're just fine," said Mrs. Butterfield. "The movers did most of the heavy lifting."

Mr. Butterfield chuckled. "Zach must have misheard us. We're not tired; we're retired. Just recently, in fact. Betty was a nurse, and I worked for the post office for nearly forty years. Began as a mail carrier before moving into management."

Mrs. Butterfield put her arm around her husband. "He started the same year we got married."

"Married forty years," Mrs. Santos said admiringly. "Congratulations. How did you two meet?"

"At a charity event for the hospital," Betty Butterfield replied. "I volunteered along with a few other nurses at a kissing booth. The money we raised went to help sick children."

Bernie Butterfield's eyes sparkled when he looked at his wife. "Best dollar I ever spent! I've been kissing her ever since."

Betty blushed as she clasped her husband's hand. "We'd better get going . . . lots of unpacking to do. It was lovely meeting all of you."

Mrs. Santos walked them to the door. "Thanks so much for stopping by. Since you're new to the neighborhood, we'd be happy to show you around anytime."

Adam nodded excitedly. "I know all the best dog-walking routes. And there's a great park nearby that Digger would love. I can show you how to get there."

The Butterfields thanked Adam and waved good-bye to the other kids. Janey and Lolli waved back.

"Thanks again for this!" Zach picked up the empty box he'd gotten earlier and spun it around in his hands. "Mulberry's going to flip his fur when he sees it."

Mr. Butterfield stroked his beard thoughtfully. "We'll probably have fifty more empty boxes when we finish unpacking. Let us know if you'd like another one. We'll take the rest to be recycled."

Janey had an idea. "You could bring them to the Third Street Animal Shelter instead. They have lots of cats—and other animals—who might like to play with boxes or sleep in them."

All four of the kids volunteered at the shelter, helping with everything from cleaning kennels and sweeping floors to feeding and grooming the animals. Some of the work was tedious, but it was all important.

"Yes!" Lolli clapped her hands in excitement. "Kitty showed me how to make a fun cat toy by cutting holes in a shoebox and hiding jingly bells inside. The shelter cats loved it. I wonder if we could make similar toys out of bigger boxes."

"Kitty is one of the workers at the shelter," Adam explained to the Butterfields. "She knows a lot about animals and how to take care of them."

"Well then, we look forward to meeting her." Mr. Butterfield thanked Janey for her suggestion, and the couple started down the walkway arm-in-arm. "Let's get started unpacking so the critters can get their paws on those boxes."

*　　*　　*

Back in Adam's room, Janey checked her in-box but there were no new messages. Since they decided to help Stacey and her hamsters, she could write a blog post about them. She decided to do some research. She opened an Internet browser and started a new search. In moments, she was clicking through pages of hamster care information. "*Aww,* how cute!" she said as she scrolled through a bunch of adorable photos.

"Finding people to adopt Stacey's hamsters shouldn't be too difficult." Lolli twirled a springy curl around her finger while she thought. "At least they're small. Anyone who loves hamsters and wants one can probably take care of one."

"Unlike a pony," Adam agreed. One of the Pet Rescue Club's most challenging cases had involved a lonely little pony named Lola.

They'd finally found a loving home for her with Mrs. Jamison, who owned a farm not far from Lolli's.

"I don't think I should have hamsters," Zach said. "Mulberry might think they're treats!"

"Roscoe's so anxious, he'd probably be afraid of a little hamster," Lolli said with a grin. Along with Mulberry, Roscoe was one of the club's official mascots. A big, lovable mutt, Roscoe was part rottweiler, part Labrador retriever, and part who-knows-what-else. "Besides, my parents won't let me have any more pets." In addition to Roscoe, Lolli's family had a sheep, two goats, and a flock of chickens on their farm.

Adam and Janey looked at each other and frowned. Both animal lovers, neither one of them had pets of their own. Adam's landlord didn't allow pets, while Janey's father was allergic to anything with fur or feathers.

Janey looked back at the photos on her screen. A smile slowly spread across her face as an idea took shape. "They are awfully small. Even if my dad is allergic, how bad could it be?"

"Probably not too bad," Lolli guessed. "They don't have very much fur."

Zach touched his temples and fluttered his eyelids. He was back in his mind-reader mode. "You're thinking about adopting one of Stacey's hamsters," he said in a trancelike tone.

"Yes." Janey nodded, grinning from ear to ear. "I can't believe I didn't think of it before. I always had my heart set on a dog or cat, but hamsters are cute and cuddly, too. And they're so tiny, I bet they won't make my father sick."

"Told you I can read minds." Zach gave her a shoulder shove.

Adam and Lolli rolled their eyes, but Janey was too excited to care about Zach's antics. "Finally, a pet of my very own," she said dreamily. "Maybe even seven!"

3

At the Shelter

The next morning, Janey woke up bright and early. It was Saturday, and she was scheduled for a volunteer shift at the Third Street Animal Shelter. First, she planned to talk to her parents about adopting the hamsters. The night before, she'd stayed awake in bed, working out in her mind exactly what she would say to persuade them. Of course, she would pay for whatever supplies her new pets needed. She'd give them fresh food and water daily and clean their cage every weekend. And she'd make sure they got plenty of exercise—she learned from the shelter that hamsters are very active animals who need to exercise every day or they would get bored, gain weight, and maybe even get sick.

When her parents came downstairs, she'd already set the table. She wanted to surprise them by making a hot breakfast, but she wasn't allowed to use the stove without an adult in the room. She could use the toaster, so she'd browned three slices of bread and placed jam on the table, along with cereal and milk.

Her mother came into the kitchen just as Janey was pouring fresh orange juice into three glasses. "How lovely! Are we celebrating a special occasion?" Mrs. Whitfield asked. "It's not my birthday or Dad's."

"It's not Mother's Day or Father's Day

either," Janey's father added, pulling out a chair.

"No, it's not a special occasion," Janey said while filling her bowl with cereal and adding milk. "I was up early because there's something on my mind. Something I want to ask you both."

"And you wanted to 'butter us up,' first?" Mr. Whitfield chuckled as he slathered butter onto a piece of toast.

Janey smiled at her father's corny joke. "Maybe a little." She took a sip of orange juice, wiped her mouth on a napkin, then told her parents about Stacey Fletcher's hamsters. Stacey had sent another e-mail last night, this time attaching photos of Hammie, Herman, and their six babies. They all had different colors and patterns on their fur. Janey couldn't decide which one was the cutest. "Stacey's parents will only let her keep one."

"So the Pet Rescue Club has to find seven homes for seven hamsters?" Mrs. Whitfield asked.

Janey bit her lip. "Actually, I was thinking . . . I was wondering if . . . maybe . . . ," Somehow the words weren't coming out the way she had practiced them. She let out a frustrated sigh.

"What is it, sweetheart?" Janey's father asked with a playful poke on her shoulder. "Cat got your tongue?"

"We don't have a cat," she reminded him. "Or a dog. But . . . we could have a hamster!" Then the words Janey had rehearsed came tumbling out. "They're so small, they hardly have any fur at all—certainly not enough to make anyone sneeze or wheeze. I'll keep them in my room, Dad, so you probably won't even notice they're here." She smiled brightly as she looked across the table at her parents.

"Oh, Janey." Her mother shook her head slowly. "You know we'd give the world to make you happy. But for people with severe allergies, like your father, even little animals can cause big problems."

Janey felt the corners of her lips tug downward.

"Hamsters have dander just like cats and dogs do," Mr. Whitfield explained. She knew that dander—tiny skin cells that are constantly shed by animals—is what causes allergic reactions in people like her father. He patted Janey's head tenderly. "I'm sorry, sweetie, but we just can't have anything—"

"Anything with fur or feathers," Janey finished his sentence. "I know, I know." She pushed her chair back from the table and carried her cereal bowl and juice glass to the kitchen sink. "I'm not very hungry. I think I'll get ready for my volunteer shift."

* * *

Volunteering at the Third Street Animal Shelter usually cheered Janey up—especially if she got to spend time cuddling cats or dogs. It was the next best thing to having a pet of her own. Some of the animals had been neglected prior to arriving at the shelter and they really seemed to enjoy the extra attention, which made Janey feel doubly good.

She wasn't sure if it would do the trick today, however. She'd gotten her hopes up about having a cute little hamster, and though she understood her parents' reason for saying no, she was still sad. She managed a weak smile for her father as he dropped her off in front of the shelter.

"Pick you up at three?" he asked as she climbed out of the car.

"Yes, Dad. Thanks."

The shelter was nestled between the post office and a floral shop. The sounds and scents of animals greeted her as she entered the lobby, a large room with animal murals painted on the walls. She found her favorite shelter worker sitting behind the front desk. "Hi, Kitty."

"Oh, hi, Janey. I was hoping you were Zach." She frowned, tucking a loose strand of blond hair back into her ponytail. "I'm sorry, that didn't come out right. I'm glad you're here. I need lots of help today, but right this minute I could really use Zach's tech skills."

Zach was practically a computer genius. He helped Janey run her blog and was good with all sorts of electronic gadgets.

Janey leaned over the desk to get a better look at the computer. The screen displayed a series of dancing zigzags. Kitty tapped the keyboard repeatedly, a frustrated grimace on her face.

At that moment, Zach strolled into the office and propped his skateboard against a wall. His mother followed close behind, carrying her medical bag. Dr. Goldman was a veterinarian with a busy practice of her own, but she volunteered her services to the shelter whenever she could. She greeted Kitty warmly and then hurried to the cat room to check on a kitten who'd come in with an ear infection.

Zach saluted Kitty, greeting her in a teasing tone, "Zach Goldman, reporting for duty."

"Perfect timing," Kitty said. "I'm trying to do a video conference with a shelter in another part of the state, but the image is scrambled. Can you fix it?"

Zach pulled a rolling chair up to the desk. "I'll give it a try."

"Great, thanks." As Zach examined the computer, Kitty turned to Janey. "I already fed the dogs, but you can help me prepare breakfast for the cats."

Janey nodded enthusiastically and started for the bins where the cat food was stored. She knew that some of the animals had special nutritional needs due to age or illness, so she reviewed a chart hanging on the wall that contained all that information. Then she assisted Kitty in filling the food bowls with the proper diet for each feline.

As they worked, Janey told Kitty about Stacey Fletcher's hamsters—and her disappointment at not being able to adopt one or two for herself. "I was hoping to keep them all at my house until I found them homes," she said, "but that's not possible either because of my father's allergies. Can they stay here at the shelter?"

"Seven hamsters?" Kitty crinkled her nose. "There's a lot to consider. First you'll have to separate them so they don't have more babies."

"Oh! I hadn't thought of that." Janey remembered how Stacey thought Hammie and Herman were both boys until their babies were born. If they continued sharing the same habitat, they'd probably have even more babies. Her eyes widened as she pictured the Pet Rescue Club trying to find homes for hundreds of hamsters. That would be a never-ending job!

She helped Kitty deliver the food bowls to each cat. Some of the cats meowed loudly upon hearing them approach. Janey smiled as an older cat named Miles rubbed against her leg when she delivered his breakfast. She bent and scratched his head, cooing, "Good boy."

"Hamsters should be housed alone or, if they get along well, in same-sex pairs," Kitty continued.

Janey frowned. "Won't they get lonely all by themselves?"

Kitty shook her head, her blond ponytail bouncing side to side. "They're solitary animals. As long as they have what they need—water and different types of food, a good habitat, and lots of opportunities to stay busy with exercise and toys to play with— they are perfectly content on their own."

Janey nodded thoughtfully. She'd recently read a book about bears and learned that they are also solitary. They live most of their lives alone—except when they are cubs and need their mother's care.

Dr. Goldman was just finishing her

exam of Sassy, a little pumpkin-colored fur ball. "His ears look much better today," she told Kitty. "I'll check him again in a couple of days. In the meantime, keep giving him the medicated ear drops I prescribed." She packed her supplies back into her medical bag. "Zach told me about the hamster project, Janey. And Kitty's right about separating them. With hamsters, it's not easy to tell boys and girls apart. I can help with that."

Janey thanked the veterinarian and continued down the row of cat kennels until she'd delivered all the meals.

"How's it going, Zach?" Kitty asked when they returned to the office. "It's almost time for my video chat."

Zach looked up from the monitor. "I updated the driver and refreshed your settings. Now I'll reboot the computer and see if it did the trick." He pressed a few keys and leaned back in the desk chair.

While they waited for the computer to restart, Kitty and Janey resumed their hamster conversation. "They can stay here," Kitty said at last. "But you kids will have to take responsibility for caring for them. We have a full house already, and we're super busy planning our upcoming Adoption Fair."

"That's great." Zach reached up and high-fived Janey. "We can all take turns on hamster duty. And we'll help out with the Adoption Fair, too."

Janey nodded in agreement. Her excitement turned quickly to worry as she remembered that they'd have to separate the hamsters. "How many habitats will we need for seven hamsters? And where will we get them?"

Kitty walked over to a storage closet, opened the door and peered inside. "Looks like we have a few spare cages you can use. We can put temporary dividers in them to create separate spaces. That should do for a short-term solution, but remember hamsters should not be kept in small cages. They need lots of space to play and explore. Of course, each section must have its own food bowl, water bottle, exercise wheel, and good bedding for sleeping."

They heard a ping and Kitty glanced at her cell phone. "It's a text from my friend at the other shelter. She's online now, waiting for me to connect."

"Almost ready," Zach said.

Kitty and Janey stood behind Zach and watched as he double-clicked the icon for the video chat program. A moment later the screen filled with the sweet, smiling face of a dog.

4

Chatting with Champion

Helping Kitty feed the shelter cats had improved Janey's mood somewhat. Now, at the sight of a big smiling dog, her spirits skyrocketed. The dog's expression was infectious; Janey felt herself grinning widely in return. "Hi there!" she said.

"I never met a dog who knew how to video chat," said Zach, laughing.

"I think he has help." Kitty smiled and pulled up a chair. "Gina? Are you there?"

They heard a human voice call over the

speakers, "Here I am!" The image shifted and a woman with long black braids came into view. She was sitting behind—or rather, underneath—the dog. "Champion climbed onto my lap just as I was logging on. He's a real show-stealer."

Kitty introduced Gina to Zach and Janey, and the kids waved in greeting.

Gina went on to explain that Champion, a three-year-old yellow Labrador retriever, was the reason she was calling. She patted the big dog's head. "This sweet fellow has been with us for a few weeks. His previous owner gave him up because he couldn't handle the expense of a special-needs animal."

"Special needs?" Janey echoed. "But he looks perfectly healthy."

"He's healthy, all right. But he has a disability." Gina adjusted her video settings, and the image on Kitty's screen zoomed out further. Now that they could see Champion's entire body, they realized the dog was missing his hind paws. His front legs were

fully formed, but his back legs were small stumps covered with bright blue socks.

Janey's heart ached for the disabled dog. How could he ever run or chase a ball or frolic in the rain? "What happened to him?"

"We believe he was born like this. He pulls himself around by his front paws, and he never seems to complain. That's how he got his name—Champion." Gina pet the dog and laughed. "Nothing keeps Champion down!"

"He seems amazing! What do you need my help with?" Kitty asked. Just then the bell over the lobby door chimed and a couple wearing matching jogging suits entered the shelter. "Hold on a minute, Gina," Kitty said into her computer's Webcam.

Janey and Zach recognized Adam's new neighbors, Mr. and Mrs. Butterfield, and introduced them to Kitty. "They just moved into town," Zach told her.

"Yes, and we have a few dozen empty moving boxes in our SUV." Mr. Butterfield gestured through the window to the vehicle parked out front. "The kids thought you could put them to good use here."

"Why, yes. We can use them for all sorts of things. Some of the animals will sleep or hide or play in them. I could use some large pieces of cardboard to make signs to advertise our upcoming Adoption Fair, too."

"Can we create cat toys like the ones you taught Lolli how to make?" Janey asked.

"Absolutely. Why don't you and Zach help carry in the boxes while I finish up my video conference." She turned back to the computer and chuckled. Champion's happy face once again filled the entire screen. He really did like to steal the show.

"You're doing a video chat with a dog?" Mrs. Butterfield said with wonder. "What will they think of next?!" She followed her husband out to the SUV, and with the kids' help they quickly transferred the boxes into the shelter's storage room.

By the time the Butterfields left, Gina had finished describing Champion's case to Kitty. "That's why we need your help," she concluded.

Zach and Janey returned in time to hear the end of Gina's plea. Since forming the Pet Rescue Club, they were always on the lookout for animals in need, so their ears instantly perked up. "Help? For Champion?" Zach asked.

"Champion may be a good candidate for prosthetics," Kitty said, explaining that prosthetic was the term for an artificial body part. "In this case, it would be his back legs. With luck, there's a chance he could walk on all fours for the first time in his life."

"I've heard about people with prosthetic arms or legs. I didn't know they made them for animals, too," Janey said.

"They do." Gina nudged Champion aside so she could be seen on the computer screen, too. "It used to be pretty rare, but now there are several firms that specialize in artificial limbs for animals. We found one that can help Champion, but it's far away from here. We're worried that the long drives to and from—for fittings, training, and physical therapy—would be very difficult for Champion. And our staff, as well. We're not sure we can manage it."

Janey was sad. She wanted to help Champion, but she couldn't think of anything the Pet Rescue Club could do. They weren't old enough to drive, so they couldn't get Champion to and from his appointments. She looked over at Zach and shrugged helplessly.

"It's too bad the prosthetics company is so far away," Zach said.

"Yes, but that brings me to the question I was about to ask Kitty." Gina's voice was coming over the speaker, but Champion was hogging the screen again. It looked like Gina's words were coming from the dog's mouth!

"I've got to capture this," Zach said, and he clicked the keys that would take a snapshot of the display. He repeated the process a few more times, then dragged all the screen grabs into a folder he created on the computer's desktop.

"The company that makes the prosthetics is far away from us," Gina continued. "But it's close to the Third Street Shelter."

Kitty raised her eyebrows in surprise. "We'd love to help Champion, but I'm not sure how . . . "

Before she could finish her sentence, Zach chimed in, "Champion should come and stay here."

"I concur!" Janey hopped up and down, unable to contain her excitement. "That way he'll be close by for his appointments.

And the Pet Rescue Club will help with his training and whatever else he needs."

"That makes sense." Kitty thought about the logistics and finally told Gina, "We'd be happy to have Champion stay here while he gets his prosthetics." She traded high-fives with Zach and Janey.

On the other end of the videoconference, Gina gave the dog a great big hug.

5

Getting Ready

"Pizza day is the best day!" Janey said as she set down her tray in the school cafeteria. She sat across from Lolli, who was unpacking her insulated lunch bag. "I know you like the healthy foods your mom packs for you, but it's too bad you have to miss out on pizza. So good . . . ," she said with a mouthful of her first bite.

"I'd die without pizza," Zach added dramatically as he and Adam took their usual places at the cafeteria table.

Lolli's parents believed in living off the

land. They grew most of their own food on the farm. "Don't be silly," she told her friends. "I eat pizza all the time. We make it with farm-grown tomatoes and cauliflower and herbs and even mushrooms." She closed her eyes and patted her stomach, picturing her mother's organic pizza. "It's delicious!"

"I'd love to try it sometime," Janey said sincerely.

"Me, too. As long as it doesn't have broccoli on it." Zach popped a piece of pepperoni into his mouth.

Adam shrugged. "I'd eat it even with broccoli on top." He liked almost every type of food. "So tell us more about Champion. I can't wait to meet him."

Zach had e-mailed Adam and Lolli the images of Champion that he'd captured during the videoconference, and they'd instantly fallen in love with the disabled dog and his winning smile. The four friends vowed to do anything they could to help him.

Zach told them that his mother had volunteered to consult on Champion's case. She'd already contacted Champion's former veterinarian and reviewed his medical records. "She says he was born with a deformity. The tendons in his feet didn't allow his legs to develop properly. The good news is he's not in any pain."

"What's the bad news?" Janey asked.

"He sometimes gets sores from dragging his back legs around. Dogs like Champion can also develop problems as they get older because they put extra pressure on their good limbs to make up for the ones that don't work. And because he can't run, he's not getting enough exercise."

Adam pushed his glasses farther back on his nose. "How long until he can get his new legs?"

Zach shrugged. "My mom said the prosthetics company can't start making them until they see Champion and take his measurements."

Janey gestured to a brown-haired girl with braces sitting at another table. "Hey, isn't that Stacey Fletcher?"

Zach followed Janey's gaze until he saw Stacey, who was covering up a yawn. "Yeah, that's our Hamster Girl."

"Gosh, she looks tired," Lolli said. "I hope she's not getting sick or something." Lolli was always concerned about other people. It was one of the things Janey admired most about her friend.

Adam finished his pizza and wiped his

mouth on a napkin. "When will Champion get here?"

Janey chimed in, "Kitty e-mailed me last night. She said Gina is planning to drive him to the Third Street Animal Shelter this week. They should arrive on Friday."

Lolli dipped a carrot stick into her veggie dip. "We should all be there, like a welcoming committee! I'll sign up to volunteer after school that day."

"Me, too," Zach said. "I promised Kitty we'd help her get the shelter ready for the Adoption Fair."

Janey nodded. "And don't forget—we have to find homes for seven hamsters."

"Eight," said an unfamiliar voice. Janey turned to see Stacey Fletcher approaching their table. They exchanged greetings, and

Lolli said, "Are you all right, Stacey? You look sleepy."

Stacey yawned. "My hamsters run on their wheels all night long. They keep waking me up."

"I've been reading a book about hamsters," Janey told the group. "They're crepuscular, which means they are active near dawn and dusk."

"I didn't know that," Adam said.

"Believe me, it's true." Stacey rubbed her tired eyes. "Anyway, I decided I don't want to keep any of them."

"Not even Hammie?" Zach asked, and Stacey shook her head sadly.

Janey reached into her backpack and pulled out a book. A chubby-cheeked hamster was pictured on the cover. "The book says that pet hamsters can adapt to a daytime schedule. Would you like to borrow it?"

Stacey took the book. "Sure, but I don't know if it will change my mind."

Janey gave her a sympathetic look. "Bring the hamsters to the Third Street Animal Shelter, and the Pet Rescue Club will find them all new homes."

"I'll ask my parents to drive me there after school today." Stacey thanked them and started to yawn again as she walked away.

"The problem with pizza is there's never enough of it," Adam said after swallowing the last bite of his slice. "Are you going to finish your carrot sticks, Lolli?"

"Help yourself." Lolli passed him the container. "I'm full."

"Thanks." As they cleared the table and

made their way out of the cafeteria, the four friends returned to the topic of Champion.

"He seems like such a happy puppy," Lolli said, smiling as she remembered the pictures Zach sent her.

"He's not a puppy," Zach replied. "He's three years old. My mom says that's a good age for getting prosthetics. He's still young enough to have lots of energy but his body is full-grown, so he won't outgrow his new legs . . . if he ever gets them."

Lolli's smile fell instantly. "What do you mean 'if'?"

Zach frowned. "According to my mom, even though the prosthetics company offered their lowest rate to help Champion, making a pair of 'bionic legs' will still cost hundreds of dollars. Gina's shelter put up a donation box, but they don't have nearly enough money."

"Why don't we help raise the money?" Adam asked as they reached their classroom. "Like we did for Maxi." Maxi was a mastiff who had received a much-needed operation thanks to the fundraising efforts of the Pet Rescue Club.

"I concur. Let's do it!" Janey said. "We have to help Champion get his new legs."

"We could hold a bake sale," Lolli suggested. "Or a pizza party."

Adam nodded excitedly, but Zach shook his head. "And have Adam eat all of our profits?" he joked. "We should sell something that's not edible!"

The others laughed and they all agreed to start brainstorming ideas for how to raise money.

"Don't forget about the hamsters," Janey reminded them. She was feeling a little worried as she took her seat and opened her math book. Finding homes for eight hamsters was a big task, and she and her friends were already busy with homework, chores, and volunteering at the shelter. Looking at the math problems on the page gave her an idea. Eight hamsters divided by four members of the Pet Rescue Club equaled two each. If each of them found homes for two hamsters they'd be done in no time. Then they could focus on raising money for Champion.

6

The Big Day

"Whoa, Ziggy, you're a bundle of energy!" Adam Santos said, smiling at the dog on the other end of his leash. Ziggy, a terrier with crazy multi-colored hair, was Adam's newest dog-walking assignment. The little dog never seemed to walk a straight line, but zagged back and forth, left and right, checking out every tree, bush, and crack in the sidewalk. She also wanted to greet every other dog they encountered along the way. Adam was always careful to ask the owners' permission before letting Ziggy approach other dogs.

They were nearing the end of Adam's block when a couple rounded the corner from the other direction. They were walking a medium-sized dog with thick tan-and-white hair. Adam recognized his new neighbors, the Butterfields, and knew the shaggy pooch at their side must be Digger. He waved and shouted hello.

Ziggy bounced up and down with excitement. Adam tightened his grip on the dog's leash. "Ziggy, sit." The little dog obeyed and Adam bent to scratch her head. "Good girl."

"Howdy, neighbor," Mr. Butterfield said with a grin. "Who's your friend?"

"This is Ziggy. She's super friendly and full of energy. And that must be Digger."

"Yes, that's our boy." Mrs. Butterfield

nodded. "He's an Australian shepherd. And he's good with other dogs, even hyper ones."

"Great, because I think Ziggy really wants to say hello." As the two dogs circled and sniffed each other, Adam filled in the Butterfields on the latest activities of the Pet Rescue Club. When he told them about the hamsters, Mrs. Butterfield grinned.

"I had a pet hamster when I was a child," she said. "I loved to watch him run on his wheel, and climb through the tunnels of his habitat."

"They are lively animals," her husband agreed.

Adam smiled as an idea took shape. "How would you like to adopt a pair of them?" Adam asked. "Two boys or two girls?"

The sparkle in Mrs. Butterfield's eyes told Adam that she liked the idea. "What do you think?" she asked her husband, who chuckled.

"Well, why not? You know I can't say no to you, my dear."

*　　*　　*

The big day was finally here. It was Friday, and Champion was due to arrive at the Third Street Animal Shelter. Janey could hardly wait for school to get out. She and her friends had gotten their parents' permission to walk to the shelter together after school. As they traveled the short distance, they chatted excitedly about Champion.

"He seems so friendly. I can't wait to give him a big hug," Janey said, and Lolli agreed.

"I can't wait to take him for his first walk," Adam said. "Once he gets his new legs."

Zach rolled along beside them on his skateboard. "First, you teach him to walk. Then I'll teach him how to riiiiide!"

Kitty was at the front desk when they arrived at the shelter. "Champion's not here yet," she said before they could even ask the question that was on their minds. "Why don't you check on the hamsters while you wait? They need fresh food and water."

Janey led the way to a small room off the lobby, where three cages were lined up on a shelf. The day after Stacey Fletcher and her parents dropped off the hamsters, Dr. Goldman had paid a visit to the shelter. She examined the hamsters, declared them all healthy, and identified each by gender. There were five boys and three girls. Later that day Kitty and Janey set up the cages using supplies they found in the storage closet and some extra hamster wheels donated by the pet store.

Adam raised the lid of the first cage and reached inside to retrieve the food bowl. A caramel-colored hamster brushed his whiskers against Adam's hand, and he chuckled. "Hammie, that tickles!"

"I'll feed the girls," Lolli said. The cage on the end was divided in half by a cardboard separator. Herman—who they'd renamed

Harriet—was on one side of the divider; her two daughters shared the other side. Lolli rinsed and refilled the water bottles on both sides of the cage and then added fresh food to the bowls.

Zach and Janey approached the largest cage, which held four male hamsters, split into two groups of two. "I talked to the family of one of my mom's patients yesterday," Zach said as he unclipped the water bottles from the side of the cage. "They want to take two of the boys."

"And don't forget the Butterfields," Adam added. "They said they'd stop by today to pick up two girl hamsters."

"That's great," Janey said. "I've been asking around, but no luck so far. What about you, Lolli?"

Lolli held up three fingers. "I talked to some of the teachers at school. Mr. Mancilla wants a hamster as a classroom pet, and apparently his wife just loves hamsters so they're going to take him home over weekends, school breaks, and for the summer. And Mrs. Kimball said she'd take two for her granddaughters."

"That's seven of the eight hamsters! Awesome!" Janey said as she high-fived each of the members of the Pet Rescue Club.

When they finished feeding the hamsters, Kitty put the kids to work prepping for the upcoming Adoption Fair. "Here's a list of signs we need," she said, pointing to a clipboard. "A few big ones to advertise and point the way to the event, and several smaller ones that say 'Adopt Me,' which we'll hang on the animal crates and corrals. Now, who's got the best handwriting?"

Zach raised his hand. "I like to draw comics, and I learned how to do lettering with all kinds of cool effects—shading and starbursts and explosions and stuff. You know, like, '*Kapow! Zap! Blam!*'"

"Sounds awesome." Kitty handed him a bin filled with nontoxic paints and markers in a variety of colors. "That'll get attention."

Janey volunteered, "I can draw cats and dogs on some of the signs. I love to draw animals."

Adam picked up a pair of scissors. "I'll start cutting pieces of cardboard for the signs."

Lolli helped Kitty organize the paperwork that prospective adopters would need to fill out before taking an animal home.

As they worked, the kids told Kitty about their plan to help Champion get his prosthetics. So far, they hadn't agreed on the best way to raise the money.

Janey was painting a cute Dalmatian puppy on one of the signs. She set down her brush and looked up at Kitty. "Could we make things to sell at the Adoption Fair?"

"That's an excellent idea," Kitty agreed. "Animal lovers sometimes stop by to support the shelter, even if they aren't ready to adopt. They might come to get some information or just make a donation."

Janey looked at the sign-making supplies and the stack of boxes donated by Adam's neighbors. "We could use the leftover boxes to make animal-related crafts."

Lolli, whose family was big on recycling, loved the idea of putting the Butterfield's moving boxes to use in a new way. "We could make cat toys! And doggie beds."

"How about hamster mazes?" Adam suggested.

"Yeah," Zach said. "And all the money we make will go to Champion's fund."

The bell over the front door tinkled and Janey leaped to her feet. "Hooray, he's here!"

The kids hurried to the door expecting to see Champion, but it was the Butterfields who entered instead. "Why look, the gang's all here," Mr. Butterfield said as he held the door open for his wife.

"Hello." Janey tried to hide her disappointment. The Butterfields were super nice, but she felt like she would go crazy waiting for Champion to arrive. What was taking him so long?

The Butterfields were pleased to learn that their old moving boxes were being turned into items whose sale would benefit a disabled dog. After catching up with Kitty and the kids, Mrs. Butterfield announced, "We've come to pick up our new hamsters. I can't wait to meet them."

"I'll get them for you," Janey said.

She'd only gone a few steps when the bell over the door jingled again. This time the sound was accompanied by a *woof*. Janey turned to see a woman with long black braids standing in the doorway. She recognized her as Kitty's friend Gina, whom she and Zach had seen on the video chat.

"Hello! Sorry we're a little late; the drive took longer than expected," Gina said. "Come on, boy." She tugged gently on a leash and a

yellow Labrador came into view, hopping on his front legs and pulling his backside behind him. Janey's heart swelled at the sight of the dog, whose smile was as bright in person as it had been over the computer screen. Champion had finally arrived!

7

Zach's Idea

"Can we pet him?" Janey asked once Gina and Champion were inside, and Kitty had made introductions all around.

Gina nodded. "I'm sure he'd like that."

"Let's bring him into the Meet-and-Greet room," Kitty said, pointing the way.

Once inside the small tiled room, Gina unclipped Champion's leash. Janey let Champion lick her hand before rubbing his head and scratching behind his ears. Then Zach, Lolli, and Adam came forward to pet and hug the dog. Soon all four kids were on the floor with Champion, who wriggled his way back and forth between them. Lolli squealed with delight as Champion hoisted himself onto her lap and licked her face.

"What a happy doggy," Mrs. Butterfield said. Intrigued by the dog, the Butterfields had followed the group into the Meet-and-Greet room and watched them play. "And so energetic!"

"What happened to him?" Mr. Butterfield asked.

Gina told them about Champion's rear-leg deformity and the plans to get him artificial hind limbs. "He'll stay here for a while, so he can be closer to the prosthetics company. Then he'll come back to the shelter where I work. That is, unless he finds a new home by then."

The Butterfields looked at each other, and both knew they were thinking the same thing: Perhaps they should adopt Champion. After a moment, Mrs. Butterfield shook her head. She told her husband, "I can't read minds any better than Zach can, but I know you're thinking about that beautiful dog. May I remind you, we've already got a dog. And two hamsters, as of today."

"Oh, the hamsters!" Janey hopped up from where she'd been playing with Champion. "I nearly forgot." Adam joined her, and in moments they returned with a small cardboard carrier. "Here they are."

Mr. Butterfield took the carrier and peeked through one of the air holes at the hamsters inside. "Yes, indeed, we do have a full house. And a boy in college who still needs his parents—well, at least once in a while! Plus, we're settling in to a new house. There's so much to do."

Gina nodded. "Champion is a very special dog. And I am certain that the right family will come along who can give him the love and attention he needs."

"We should stop by the pet store on the way home and pick up a few things for our new pets," Mrs. Butterfield said to her husband.

"I had the exact same idea, my dear," Mr. Butterfield said. "Being married forty years is even better than being a mind reader," he told Zach with a wink.

Gina watched the Butterfields depart. "What a lovely couple. Married forty years and still acting like sweethearts."

"That's it!" Zach shouted. "I have the perfect fundraising idea for Champion."

Janey shook her head in confusion. "What do you mean?"

"Do you remember how Mr. and Mrs. Butterfield met?" Zach asked.

"At a kissing booth for charity," Adam answered. "He paid a dollar to kiss her and the money went to help sick kids. But you aren't suggesting we should have a kissing booth." His cheeks turned bright red at the thought. "Are you?"

"Gross!" Lolli and Janey said in unison.

Seeing his friends' shocked expressions, Zach chuckled. "No, no. It won't be that kind of kissing booth. For a dollar donation, people can get a cuddle from Champion. We can call it a Cuddle Booth."

The kids looked at Champion, who was enjoying a belly rub from Kitty. Seeing the dog's joyful expression, Janey had to admit

Zach's idea was a good one. Who wouldn't pay a dollar to put a smile on Champion's face—especially if the money went to a good cause? And she could think of no better cause than helping Champion finally run and play like other dogs.

*   *   *

Kitty gave the Cuddle Booth idea a thumbs-up. Then she and Gina brought Champion to the dog room, where he immediately started greeting his neighbors—a schnauzer and a dachshund—through the bars of his kennel. He seemed curious and confident, signs that he would adjust well to his new surroundings. Once satisfied that the dog was in good hands, Gina left the shelter, promising to keep in close touch with the team about Champion's progress.

When she returned to the front lobby, Kitty found that Adam and Lolli had taken over the poster-making duties, while Zach and Janey were huddled over the computer.

"I wrote a blog post about the Adoption Fair," Janey told her. Janey had started the blog Janey's Pet Place as a way to get people to share cute animal pictures. Now, the Pet Rescue Club also used the blog to get the word out about animals in need.

Kitty read the blog post over Janey's shoulder. "This is great. Hopefully it will get more people to come to the fair."

Janey nodded. "I'm going to add information about the Cuddle Booth. Check out the video Zach made."

With a few mouse clicks, Zach opened a video player. The words "Smooch This

Pooch" appeared above Champion's smiling face as he licked the camera. Zach pointed to a flashing icon on the video screen. "When someone clicks this link, it takes them to Janey's blog post about Champion and why we are raising money for him."

"I included information about disabled dogs and prosthetics and stuff," Janey said.

Lolli and Adam came over to check out the video. "Aww," Lolli said as the clip replayed

on a loop. "Who could resist that face? I'll bet people will line up to smooch Champion."

Adam agreed. "And we'll raise enough money to pay for his prosthetics!"

8

Adoption Fair

The weather was breezy and warm, the perfect day for an Adoption Fair. The staff and volunteers of the Third Street Animal Shelter had set up the event in a nice shady section of the park. Balloons and banners decorated the area, which included information booths and several enclosures where animals seeking adoption were corralled. People milled about, checking out the dogs and cats on display.

Sassy, the pumpkin-colored kitten who had been cured of her ear infection, was being cuddled by a boy with glasses and brown hair. "This one! Can we have this one?" he asked his parents. As Kitty talked to the family about Sassy, Janey set up a sign that read HAMPSTER FOR ADOPTION in front of a nearby table where she sat with Hammie.

Hammie was the last of Stacey Fletcher's hamsters available for adoption. Dr. Goldman's patient had picked up a pair of boys earlier in the week, and Lolli and Janey had delivered Harriet and two other boys to their teachers Mr. Mancilla and Mrs. Kimball. Several people had stopped by Janey's table to admire Hammie, but most had come to the fair hoping to adopt a dog or a cat. She'd been there for more than an hour, and was beginning to worry that Hammie would never find a new home.

Lolli sat at a long table, selling pet crafts

made from the Butterfield's donated boxes. "All proceeds benefit the animals of the Third Street Animal Shelter," she told interested shoppers.

A girl with long brown hair and braces approached Lolli, holding one of the custom-made crafts. "What is this thing?"

Lolli recognized Stacey Fletcher from school. "It's a hamster maze. Isn't it cool?" She showed Stacey how she'd added dividers and walls to a cardboard box to create a fun toy for hamsters. "You set them down here, and they have to find their way to the snack over here. If they reach a dead-end, they have to turn around and try another route."

"Neat," Stacey said. "So it helps them get exercise and also challenges them to figure out the puzzle."

Lolli nodded. "Hey, you're not yawning anymore. You must feel better now that your hamsters are gone."

Stacey looked down at the ground. "Yeah, I guess. I'm sleeping better, but . . . I miss Hammie. He really was a good pet."

"Well, you can see him," Lolli said, pointing across the way toward Janey. "He's right over there."

*   *   *

Adam and Zach manned the Cuddle Booth, which had a long line thanks to Janey's blog. Most of their customers told the boys they had read about Champion online and wanted to meet the dog and make a donation. Adam collected the money while Zach looked after Champion, making sure he didn't get tired or stressed. The big dog seemed happy to greet each person in line, never tiring of the attention. Often a Cuddle Booth customer approached Champion with a frown, asking if the dog was in pain. They expressed sympathy for his disability, but after spending time with the dog, they always left with a smile.

"Howdy, neighbor," Bernie Butterfield said, placing two dollar bills in front of Adam. "We came to see Champion again."

"Yes," his wife added with a smile. "I'd really like to smooch that big sweet pooch."

"Isn't he the greatest?" Adam said, looking over his shoulder at the dog, who was enjoying a cuddle from a little girl with blond pigtails. "I didn't expect to see the two of you at the Adoption Fair."

"And why not?" Mr. Butterfield asked.

"We may have a full house, but we'd still like to support the shelter. And we like to think we might have inspired this Cuddle Booth."

"That's true. Zach thought of it after you told us how you two first met." Adam put their money into his cash box. "Have you finished setting up your house yet?"

"Oh heavens, yes," Mrs. Butterfield

answered. "It's amazing how much time you have to accomplish things once you retire. We're already getting bored!"

The couple waited their turn while the little girl's mother took a photo of her daughter embracing Champion. Zach photographed the pair with his own camera, then asked the mother for permission to post the picture on Janey's Pet Place blog. "Of course," the woman answered. "Especially if it will help the shelter."

*   *   *

"Don't worry, we'll find you a new home." Janey peered into the hamster habitat at Hammie, who was nestled inside an empty paper towel tube. "Maybe not today, but soon. The Pet Rescue Club always comes through." A few families had stopped by Janey's table in the last hour, but none wanted to adopt Hammie. Janey's heart sank as she wondered if Hammie would be the first animal the Pet Rescue Club failed to help.

"Can I pet him?" someone asked.

Janey looked up to see Stacey Fletcher standing in front of her. "Of course."

Stacey reached into the cage and smiled when Hammie emerged from the tube to rub his whiskers against her fingers. "I read the book about hamsters that you loaned me. I learned a lot of neat things. Like how they load up their cheeks with food during the day and empty them out at night when they want a snack."

"I read that, too. I remember thinking that Adam would love to do the same thing!"

Janey told her about the people who'd

adopted the rest of the hamsters and promised to keep looking until they found a home for Hammie.

Stacey withdrew her hand from Hammie's cage and turned away. "Thanks for everything, Janey," she said sheepishly.

Seeing how sad Stacey looked as she walked away gave Janey an idea. "Wait," she called after the fifth grader. "Maybe we shouldn't find Hammie a new home."

"Huh?" Stacey asked, confused. "Why not?"

"I think Hammie belongs at his old home. With you."

A smile inched its way across Stacey's face as she realized Janey was right. Hammie should come home with her. She'd make it work! They talked some more and Stacey

thanked Janey and the Pet Rescue Club for their help. She purchased one of Lolli's hamster mazes and left the fair determined to be the best possible hamster parent.

An hour later, the fair was winding down. Several of the shelter animals had been matched with new owners. After sending Hammie home with Stacey, Janey helped Lolli at the craft booth until all they'd sold all the items.

"I wonder how much we made?" Lolli asked.

Janey lifted the cash jar off the table. "Feels heavy." She gave it a little shake. Both girls smiled at the sound of coins clinking against the glass. "Hear that, Lolli? It sounds like a million bucks!"

Lolli laughed. "Well, maybe not a million, but I hope it will help Champion. Let's go find Kitty."

They found her at the Cuddle Booth, adding up the donations Adam and Zach had collected. When she was done counting, Lolli turned over the craft money and they all waited nervously for the final tally. They'd worked hard, but what if it wasn't enough?

Finally, Kitty counted the last coin. She looked up at them. "Great job! You raised enough money to pay for Champion's prosthetics!"

9

New Shoes

"It's just like trying on a new pair of shoes." Janey stroked Champion's fur as he lay on his side on a metal exam table. The dog was being fit for his new prosthetic limbs. Since they'd worked so hard to raise the money to pay for them, Zach's mother knew the four club members would want to be there for the fitting. She'd driven them to the prosthetics office and introduced them to the specialist, Mr. Mascaro, a tall thin man with a kind smile who was just as taken with Champion as everyone else.

"That's right, Janey," Mr. Mascaro replied. "This one seems a little tight. So we'll go up a size. For a prosthetic to be comfortable, there should be a little bit of wiggle room. Same with a good pair of shoes." He fit an artificial limb over Champion's left hind leg and showed the kids how to fasten it properly. Then he repeated the process on the right side. "Now let's see if he can tolerate standing."

Dr. Goldman and the specialist lifted Champion off the table and placed him on the floor. They stood on either side of the dog to provide support. Champion wriggled his backside and let out a yelp. "Steady, boy," Dr. Goldman said in a reassuring tone.

The prosthetics were made out of a special plastic. Foam padding sat between the artificial limb and Champion's body.

"I've gotten used to seeing Champion with just two legs," Zach said.

Champion wriggled some more.

"He seems eager to try them out," said Mr. Mascaro. "Let's give him some room."

Everyone backed away except Dr. Goldman, who gave the yellow Lab a few strokes on the head before stepping to one side. "You can do it, Champion."

Janey could feel her heart pounding in her chest. They'd waited so long for this moment. She held her breath, waiting for Champion to take his first steps. But the dog didn't move. He seemed frozen in place.

Adam pulled a small pouch out of his pocket and removed a dog treat. Kneeling, he held the treat out toward Champion. "Come, boy."

Champion whined and then skittered forward, taking a few wobbly steps in Adam's direction.

"You can do it, Champion," Adam encouraged the dog. "Walk toward me."

Lolli clapped her hands. "He's really walking!"

The dog stopped suddenly and began twitching his hips. He kicked out with one of his rear legs, then the other. Janey's brow furrowed with concern. It seemed like Champion was trying to shake off his new legs. Dr. Goldman reached out to steady the dog.

Then Champion plopped to the floor and began chewing at the straps.

"Oh no," Janey gasped. "I think he's trying to take them off."

The specialist crouched down next to Champion. "Yes, he's telling us he's had enough for now." He began unfastening the artificial limbs. "Don't worry, kids. Champion's reaction is perfectly normal. He's not used to having hind legs, so it will take some time for him to adjust." He returned the prosthetics to their case. "And remember, these are not Champion's new shoes—they're samples that we tried out to see how they fit. Now that I've examined Champion and taken measurements, we can build a pair of legs that will fit him precisely."

As Janey absorbed this information, she looked at Champion where he lay panting on the floor. For the first time since she'd met him, the dog did not appear to be smiling. Instead he looked tired and sad. She bent down to pet him and he let out a low whimper. She sighed. "If he doesn't like wearing the prosthetics, maybe we shouldn't make him. I mean, he gets around fine without them, right? He's not in any pain, and he's one of the happiest dogs I've ever known."

"He'll get the hang of it," Zach said. "First time I rode my skateboard I fell off after a few seconds."

Lolli shook her head. "Maybe Janey's right. We all want Champion to walk on four legs, but what if that's not what he wants? Maybe we should let him stay just the way he is."

Adam gazed down at the dog. "He does look pretty pooped."

"Walking takes a lot of energy if you haven't really done it before," Mr. Mascaro said. "He'll build up his strength in no time."

Dr. Goldman put both hands on her hips as she looked at the four kids. "It's true, Champion has gotten along fine without back legs so far. His medical records show that as a puppy he was very active and agile. Now that he's full grown, the weight of his body is more difficult to drag around. He gets sores sometimes. His method of locomotion—the way he moves—also puts extra strain on his spine. That can cause big problems as he gets older." Her voice took a serious tone as she met Janey's gaze. "Walking on all fours could help him live a longer, healthier life."

Janey thought about it for a moment. Dr. Goldman's comments made sense. As hard as it was to see Champion struggle, she had to think of what was best for the dog. "Even if he doesn't like them right now, Champion needs his new shoes," she said, looking at her friends for confirmation.

Lolli said, "I agree," and Adam flashed a thumbs-up. "Me, too."

"I don't agree," Zach said. Then he added with a laugh, "I concur!"

"I wish I could have been there." Gina's face filled Kitty's computer screen. They were doing another video chat, only this time Champion was on the other side of the connection, surrounded by Janey, Zach, and Kitty. The yellow dog still liked to steal the show; he hopped up on Janey's lap and leaned in close to the Webcam, crowding everyone else out of the picture.

After they had left the prosthetics office, Dr. Goldman had driven Champion and the kids back to the Third Street Animal Shelter. Lolli's parents were already waiting to pick her up, and Adam's mother had arrived soon after.

Janey called her house and spoke to her father. "Zach's mom said she can drop me off on their way home, since our house is just a block from theirs," she told him.

"All right, sweetheart, we'll see you soon," he said before hanging up.

Now, Dr. Goldman was in the dog room, checking on Tank, a greyhound with a limp foot, and Layla, a golden retriever who'd been acting lethargic. While they waited for her to finish, Zach and Janey told Kitty and Gina all about their day—including Champion's disappointing first steps.

"Then he's just like the rest of us," Gina said. "No one walks perfectly the first time around. We crawl and stumble and fall. It takes time and practice."

"He has to do exercises to strengthen his hips and legs," Janey said. "We learned how to help him with those. We'll work with him a few minutes every day." On the car ride back, they'd worked out a schedule of who would be responsible for helping Champion exercise each day of the week.

"Mr. Mascaro also taught us how to put on and take off the prosthetics, and how to keep them clean," Zach explained. "And some things to look out for, like signs of irritation on Champion's skin. It's a lot to remember."

"Caring for a dog with special needs takes extra time and attention," Kitty agreed. "Now you know why it's important that we find the right home for Champion."

Janey put her arms around Champion's neck and nodded. She knew it would take special people to properly care for this very special dog. And the Pet Rescue Club would work extra hard to find them.

10

Three Cheers for Champion

"We can't start yet!" Janey waved her arms. "Adam's not here. He wanted to take Champion for his first walk."

"Well, where is he?" Zach asked, his voice impatient. They'd been preparing for this day for weeks. The four club members had taken turns guiding the dog through his daily training exercises. The day before, Dr. Goldman and Kitty had brought Champion for his final fitting. Now, they were all gathered at the town park, eager to see the dog try out his brand new, custom-made prosthetics. Everyone, that is, but Adam. "You don't think he forgot, do you?" Zach asked.

Janey shook her head. "No way."

"There he is!" Lolli pointed across the park to where Adam was hurrying toward them, waving something in his outstretched hand.

"I stopped at the pet store to pick this up," he said when he caught up to them. "I had it personalized." He held out a collar embroidered with the name "Champion" in bold letters. He fastened it around the dog's neck and attached a leash. "Now he's all set."

Dr. Goldman watched as Janey and Zach secured the dog's prosthetics. "Good job. Now let's help him stand."

This time, Champion didn't whimper or whine. He wagged his tail and strained at his leash as though eager to get moving.

Kitty stroked the dog's fur. "Hold on, boy." She turned to Adam. "Remember to go slowly. You don't want to overstress him on his first real walk."

Adam nodded. "Right. Like Mr. Mascaro said, walking takes a lot of energy if you're not used to it."

Zach pulled a camera out of his pocket and powered it on. "I'm going to record this for the blog. "Lights, camera . . . action!"

Kitty released Champion and the dog took off running. Adam jogged behind him, gripping the leash. "Slow down, boy. Take it easy!"

The others watched with amazement as Champion and Adam circled around one side of the park and headed back toward them. Champion's head bobbed and his tail wagged like crazy. Even from a distance, Janey could see the dog was sporting a huge smile.

Zach whistled. "Look at him go! Looks like he was born to run."

"He didn't wobble one bit," Lolli added.

Janey grinned at her friends. "Guess he just needed the right pair of shoes."

* * *

Adam was relieved when Champion slowed to a walk. He needed to catch his breath, and he was sure the dog must be tired, too. Sprinting across the park took a big burst of energy. But Champion didn't appear to be stressed; his gait was steady and strong.

As they passed under the shade of a large oak tree, Adam heard someone call out, "Howdy, neighbor!" He turned to see the Butterfields a short distance behind him, walking Digger.

"Champion's looking good," Mrs. Butterfield said as they approached. Digger and Champion sniffed each other in greeting, tails wagging. "How long has he had his prosthetics?"

"About ten minutes," Adam answered. "This is his very first walk."

"He's a remarkable animal," Mr. Butterfield said. The Butterfields and Digger fell into step beside Adam and Champion as they walked across the park. "In fact, we've been talking about him."

"Three cheers for Champion!" Lolli jumped up and down, her springy curls bouncing as she greeted the dog's return.

Janey added, "He ran like a pro."

"It was a great start." Dr. Goldman took Champion's leash from Adam. "Until he's accustomed to them, he should only wear his prosthetics for a short time each day."

"One more thing to remember." Zach turned to Kitty. "Boy, you were right about special animals needing extra care."

Kitty nodded. "That's why it's important we find him the right home." The shelter had received dozens of calls and e-mails from people interested in adopting Champion, but so far none had been the right fit. Some were from people with busy jobs or young children, who didn't realize the time commitment involved with a special needs animal.

"About that . . . ," Adam said. "I think I've found a super match for Champion. They have lots of time and energy, and they love animals."

Lolli leaned forward. "Who? Tell us!"

"No, don't tell." Zach's hands flew to his temples. "I'll read your mind." He fluttered his eyelids and spoke in a deep, trancelike tone. "It's . . . Mr. and Mrs. Butterfield."

"Really?" Janey looked to the couple for confirmation.

Mrs. Butterfield nodded excitedly. "It's true. Since retiring we realized we have plenty of free time, and we'd love to spend it with Champion. He's an inspiration."

"We've been thinking about it for a while," Mr. Butterfield added. "The only question was whether Digger would approve."

Zach looked at the two dogs, who were laying next to each other companionably. "Looks like he approves."

"So do we," Janey added. "And since you live next door to Adam, we can see

Champion all the time!"

"Three cheers for Champion," Lolli repeated, and the rest of the group joined in the celebration.

Mr. Butterfield winked at his wife and added, "Three cheers for the Pet Rescue Club!"

The Right Dog for the Right Home

There are lots of dog breeds out there—and countless adorable mixed breed dogs as well. It can be tempting to choose the cutest dog, or the friendliest, or one that reminds you of a dog from TV or the movies. But it's important to make sure the dog you adopt fits your personality and lifestyle. Do you spend a lot of time outdoors, or prefer quieter pastimes? Do you live in the country or the city? Do you like to keep your house spotless, or will a little—or a lot—of dog hair not bother you? Are you confident enough to handle a dominant breed, or do you prefer someone sweet and easygoing?

All of these questions and more are important to consider. Talk to your local shelter workers about finding the right match, or check out the many resources online to help narrow it down.

ASPCA's "Meet Your Match" program

http://www.aspca.org/adopt/meet-your-match

Good luck finding your perfect pooch—and your happily ever after!

Meet the Real Champion

Champion, the resilient pup, was inspired by a real-life animal rescue story! A sweet white dog named Margot arrived at an animal shelter in Brooklyn, New York, and was missing both of her hind feet. No one knew what had happened to her, but they knew she had been this way since she was a puppy. Fortunately for Margot, Dr. Lori Bierbrier, an ASPCA Veterinarian, and her husband Thomas and daughter Brooke got involved. Lori noticed that Margot lacked adequate "footwear," so she made booties for Margot. Even though their home was "pet full," they decided there was room for one more, and adopted Margot and had her fitted for custom prosthetics. Now Margot walks through the neighborhood with ease, just like Champion!

Look for these other books in the
PET RESCUE CLUB
series!

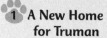 **A New Home for Truman**

2 No Time for Hallie

3 The Lonely Pony

4 Too Big to Run

 5 A Puppy Called Disaster